POSY BATES, AGAIN!

Also by Helen Cresswell

Meet Posy Bates
Time Out
Moondial
The Secret World of Polly Flint
Dear Shrink
The Piemakers
A Game of Catch
The Winter of the Birds
The Bongleweed
The Beachcombers
Up the Pier
The Night Watchmen

THE BAGTHORPE SAGA
Ordinary Jack
Absolute Zero
Bagthorpes Unlimited
Bagthorpes v. the World
Bagthorpes Abroad
Bagthorpes Haunted
Bagthorpes Liberated

POSY BATES, AGAIN!

by Helen Cresswell

illustrated by Kate Aldous

MACMILLAN PUBLISHING COMPANY
New York

MAXWELL MACMILLAN INTERNATIONAL
New York   Oxford   Singapore   Sydney

For Thea, with love

First North American edition ©1994
Text copyright © 1991 by Helen Cresswell
Illustrations copyright © 1991 by Kate Aldous

Macmillan Publishing Company is part of the
Maxwell Communication Group of Companies.

Macmillan Publishing Company
866 Third Avenue, New York, NY 10022

Printed in the United States of America
10 9 8 7 6 5 4 3 2 1
The text of this book is set in 13 point ITC Garamond Light.

Library of Congress Cataloging-in-Publication Data
Cresswell, Helen.
Posy Bates, Again! / by Helen Cresswell ; illustrated by Kate Aldous.
— 1st ed., 1st American ed.
p.   cm.
Summary: Posy Bates and her stray dog, Buggins, seem to get
into nothing but mischief no matter how good their intentions are.
ISBN 0-02-725372-4
[1. Family life—Fiction.   2. Dogs—Fiction.]
I. Aldous, Kate, ill.   II. Title.
PZ7.C8645Po 1994   [Fic]—dc20   93-5789

Contents

Posy Bates and a Dog

"Now listen, Fred," said Posy Bates. "This is the most important thing I've ever told you."

Fred, newly bathed and bottled, gazed pinkly back at her.

"It's very, very important. Mega important."

Fred hiccuped and stuck his thumb in his mouth. Normally, Posy would have pulled it straight out again. She did not approve of thumb sucking. Daff, their mother, said she liked to see it. She thought Fred looked absolutely adorable sucking his thumb; she'd gone into raptures about it.

"You won't like it when he ends up looking like Dracula," Posy would tell her, "or at the very least like Toby Rattle."

Everyone knew that Toby Rattle's teeth stuck out like a fringe because he'd sucked his thumb when he was a baby.

Now Posy itched to pull that thumb out, but didn't.

If she did, Fred would yell and not listen to a single word she was saying.

"It's life or death," she continued. "Now listen. In a bit, I'm going to show you something. Something alive. It's not a stick insect or a spider. And it's not a hedgehog. Remember the hedgehog, and what I told you about the prickles and the fleas?"

Fred made a murmuring sound that might, or might not, have showed he remembered. Posy was training her baby brother to be a genius. She gave him daily lectures on all kinds of things, from Bible stories to hedgehogs—illustrated lectures, if she could manage it.

"What this thing is," Posy told him, "is a"—she paused, because it was simply unbelievable that such a thing was possible—"is a . . . dog. D-O-G, dog."

She looked at where the D-O-G was lying, and thought she might actually burst with pride and pleasure. She had attached an old clothesline to the chain around his neck and tied him to an apple tree. Now he was lying, head between his great pudding paws, and looking at her—she felt sure. (She could not be certain because of all the fur.) It seems like a dream, but it's a dream come true, she thought. Magic.

He had been at their house for about two hours now, having appeared out of nowhere at Posy's Great

Green Pet Show. Some people would say he was a stray. Not Posy. She knew that he had been sent especially for her. She knew this because:

1. she had always wanted a dog more than anything else in the world, and
2. because he was exactly, absolutely, totally the kind of dog she had always imagined, and therefore
3. she had recognized him at first sight, and
4. he had recognized her at first sight.

She dragged her eyes away from him and back to Fred.

"A dog," she told him, "is absolutely the best kind of animal there is. It's got fur and four legs and a tail. It's a bit like a cat, only better. Cats don't wag their tails."

Fred's eyelids seemed to be drooping; he sucked blissfully. If she didn't look out, he'd be asleep before she'd finished.

"Now listen. I've actually got a dog. But the thing is, Mom won't let me keep him if *you* don't like him. So later on, when she brings you in after your nap, I'm going to show him to you. I'll tell you what he looks like, so you won't be too surprised. He's quite big—more than twice as big as you—and he's mostly black and furry. He might snuffle at you with his nose. Are you listening?"

Fred's eyes were glazed and dreamy.

"He might snuffle, and he might actually lick you with his tongue. If he does, it's a *very good sign*. It shows he likes you. The thing is, nobody's ever licked you before, so you might yell."

She gazed anxiously down at Fred. If he *did* yell, that was it. Her dog would go. How could she make sure . . . ? One of her perfect ideas floated into her mind. (Posy often had perfect ideas—they came clear out of the blue.)

She leaned over the baby carriage. First she took one of his tiny curled fists and, very gently, licked it. It was a curious feeling. Posy had never licked anyone before.

"Now your face."

She went deep in under the hood and licked Fred's warm, milky-smelling cheeks. She kept it up for quite a long time. The dog probably would, and in any case she quite enjoyed the sensation. In future, she thought, I'll lick Fred more often.

When she withdrew, Fred was asleep. Posy was enchanted. What if he went to sleep when the dog licked him? That would go down very well with Daff. She'd decide to keep the dog as a resident putter-to-sleeper. A lullaby on four legs, Posy thought, and giggled.

She went over and sat beside the dog. He raised an eyebrow but did not stir.

Used to me already, she thought.

Here came Pippa, her older sister, all dolled up. She'd been trying to spike her hair, and it stuck up all around her head like a badly painted halo. Posy wondered how she'd gotten past Daff.

"Fred asleep?"

Posy nodded. She did not mention the licking. She felt sure that Pippa, who wasn't interested in either babies or dogs, would not understand.

"You do *like* my dog?" she begged, nevertheless. She would need all the allies she could get if she was to keep him.

"All right, I s'pose. Mom'll never let you keep it."

She had voiced Posy's own darkest fear.

"She might."

"She won't."

"I'll tell you what," Posy said. "You back me up about the dog, and I'll back you up over the earrings."

"Much good *that'll* do," said Pippa sourly.

Just as Posy had always longed for a dog, so Pippa dreamed of having her ears pierced. She spent hours in shops and markets, hanging over multicolored hoops and dripping gold tassels. She already had a box full of them; enough, she had told Posy, to wear a different pair every day for a month.

Posy did not see how having her ears pierced would change her life in the way Pippa seemed to think it would. It seemed to her a very tame ambition. You couldn't train earrings to sit up and beg or sniff out bones.

"Tell Mom he'll be a good guard dog," Posy urged. "Tell her you get nightmares about burglars."

"That lump of fur wouldn't know a burglar if it tripped over one," Pippa said. "In any case, I'm not scared of burglars, Jenny Parker's teaching me ju-jitsu. I'd just pick him up and throw him over my shoulder."

Posy winced. She had just been thrown by Vicky Wright's donkey, and was beginning to feel the bruises coming out. The only *good* thing about this accident was that it had made Daff feel sorry for Posy—and that meant the dog might be allowed to stay.

"Well, you could tell Mom how good it'd be to have a guard dog, all the same," Posy urged. "And I'll say that if you have your ears pierced, it stops you from getting rheumatism."

Pippa stared. "Rheumatism?"

"Well, it does if you wear those copper bracelets. Old Mrs. Kettleborough told me," Posy said. "And I expect copper earrings do just as well."

"I'm not ninety," Pippa told her.

"All right," said Posy. "I'll wash all the dishes for you for a week if you'll stick up for me."

Pippa hesitated.

"Two weeks!" said Posy recklessly. She would have washed the dishes for a year, for life, if need be.

"Oh, all right. But you needn't think I'm taking it for walks."

"Oh, thanks! Oh, Pips, it'll be *brilling!*"

"Don't call me Pips."

"I won't, I won't! Oh, thank you!"

She limped over to the dog now and sat, gingerly, on the warm grass. His tail stirred, then, as she plunged her fingers into the thick fur on his back, went into a full-scale wag.

"Mom said you ought to be in bed," Pippa told her.

"I'm convoluting in the sun," said Posy.

"You're *what?*" Pippa stared, then went abruptly

into great squawks of laughter. Pippa had a very unfortunate laugh, Posy thought. It was lucky she didn't use it often. "You mean *convalescing!* Oh, wait till I tell Miss Gisborne!"

Miss Gisborne was Pippa's teacher and, according to her, perfect. Her first name was Tracey and she had pierced ears and frizzed chestnut hair. Posy watched her sister teeter down the path to the gate.

"I said convoluting," Posy told the dog, "and I meant convoluting. I'll look it up in the dictionary when I go in."

Posy Bates was very interested in words. She often looked them up—and made them up, too, if she felt like it.

She lay flat. The sun felt good on her aches; her whole body was one big ache. She wondered if this was what rheumatism felt like, and whether she should ask to borrow Mrs. Kettleborough's copper bracelet. Daff had said she was lucky not to have broken every bone in her body. At the moment it felt rather as if she had.

"Posy! Posy, are you all right?"

Posy opened her eyes—only a fraction because of the sun—and saw Daff standing over her.

"I've brought you some Ovaltine."

"Oh—thanks, Mom." Posy eased herself first onto

one elbow, then sat up. Her head spun and she closed her eyes again.

"*Are* you all right? You ought to be in bed!"

Posy opened her eyes, then stretched out a hand for the mug. Daff always made Ovaltine when someone was poorly. She was a great believer in it. She said it built you up. Just now, Posy felt rather in need of building up.

"I've called the police," Daff said.

"I thought it was only car accidents you had to tell them, not donkeys."

"About the dog."

"What for? He hasn't done anything!"

"He's a stray," Daff said. "He must belong to somebody. You have to report it to the police."

Posy felt suddenly cold, despite the sun and the Ovaltine. The police could arrive at any moment and take the dog away. Or the real owner, who would snap on a leash and take him off, and that would be that. She shivered.

"They said no one'd reported it missing yet. But it's early."

This was good news. If Posy had a dog like that, number one, she'd take good care not to lose him in the first place, and number two, if she ever did, she'd call the police the minute she realized he was gone.

"They said we could hang on to him if we like, or they'd take him to the SPCA."

This was bad news. Posy could guess what her mother would want to do.

"I—I don't think he'd like it much at the SPCA," she said.

"And I don't think I'll like it with that great thing under my feet all day," Daff said. "And I know you, Posy. You'll go getting fond of it, and then when its owners do turn up, there'll be tears."

There certainly would, Posy thought. Oceans and oceans of tears.

"You don't like seeing poor dumb things in cages," Posy said cunningly.

"No, I don't."

"But that's what he'd be at the SPCA. They're all in cages."

"There's Fred to think of," said Daff.

"I think he'll like Fred," Posy said. "And I think Fred'll like him."

If not, all that licking would have gone to waste.

"You get off there, little monkey!" Daff screeched suddenly.

Posy's head went fizzy again. All at once the fur disappeared from under her fingers. She saw a streak of black and a streak of ginger. The dog was chasing away the Posts' cat.

"Well! That does it! Little monkey—only put those plants in last week!"

The dog had scored a point. He had chased away Barry, who was the bane of Daff's life. He was ever-lastingly on the Bateses' side of the fence, scratching at her seedlings. She was forever rapping on the window at him, chasing him, and even hurling stones at him.

"*That* was good, Mom!" Posy said. "If he stays, your seeds'll be safe as houses. Good dog, good boy!"

One point to the dog, she added silently.

He was back, wagging his tail, and slumped beside her again.

Posy was actually quite fond of Barry, despite his exceedingly silly name. Mrs. Post had named him after some TV star or other. Posy was glad she wasn't *her* mother, or she'd probably have ended up being called Kylie or Cilla or something.

"Well, that *was* useful," Daff admitted. "Gave that darned cat something to think about."

"He'd be really handy, Mom."

The fur disappeared from under her fingers again. Surely Barry wasn't back already? The dog was barking furiously. George's van was drawing up outside the house. There was growling now. Posy's heart plummeted.

Dog, one; Mom, one, she thought.

It looked as if the points had evened out already. She could see her father's bewildered face peering out of the van window. Then, amazingly, she heard her mother laugh.

"Chase him away!" she shouted. "That's right—chase him away!"

Posy prized herself painfully to her feet. If the dog bit George (not that she believed he would in a million years), it was all over.

"Here!" she called. "No! Here!"

The trouble was, she didn't know his name. It was not easy giving orders to a dog without a name.

"Here, boy!"

The dog had stopped barking and growling. He was watching George, and George, from the safety of his van, was watching him.

"It's all right, Dad!"

"What's all this, then? Who's this?"

"You're not frightened of that great, soft thing, George!" said Daff. She was still laughing.

"He got left behind at the pet show, Dad, and he's right as rain and doesn't bite, honest!"

Posy fervently hoped that this was true.

George edged open the van door.

"Good boy!" he said. "Good old boy!"

Posy held her breath. Her father stretched out a hand. Posy shut her eyes.

"That's a good boy!"

She opened her eyes. George's hand was still there, patting the dog, and the dog's tail was wagging. Her father looked mightily pleased with himself, as if he had just tamed a man-eating tiger.

"Nice little chap," he remarked. "Got left behind, you say?"

"Stray," Daff told him. "I've phoned the police. My word, he nearly chased *you* away, George!"

"If Dad'd been a burglar, he'd have chased him away, all right!" Posy said. "He's a real guard dog. He'd never let anyone steal Fred."

Daff's eyes went automatically to the carriage, where Fred, the apple of her eye, slumbered under the apple trees.

"That's true," she murmured.

Posy adjusted the score. Dog, two; Daff, zero.

"Dad, Vicky Wright's donkey threw me—well, not exactly threw me; more like scraped me off!"

"Oooh, don't!" Daff moaned. "Honestly, George, when I saw that child go flying—oh, my heart stopped, I swear it did!"

Posy was pleased by this remark. She would never have guessed that she could have had such an effect on Daff. Usually she was nagged and told off so much that she wondered whether her mother liked her, even—let alone loved her.

"No bones broken?" said George. He patted Posy's head as though she, too, were a dog. "All right, are we, missy?"

He only ever called her that when she was feeling poorly or when he was especially pleased with her. Apparently that's what he'd called her when she was a baby, and he couldn't quite shake off the habit. He was very set in his ways, Daff said.

"I ache a bit," Posy told him. "In fact, I ache a lot."

This was true, but she'd have said it, anyway. The more sympathy she got, the more likely Daff was to let her keep the dog.

Posy had worked out long ago that grown-ups tended to be kinder to you when you weren't well. They made the kind of fuss they only usually made when you'd done something good or clever. It was enough to tempt you to be an invalid for life.

"I'm keeping an eye on her," Daff was telling George. "She might've got delayed concussion."

"I won't die, will I?" Posy asked.

Whenever anybody died in a movie, Daff did a lot of sniffing, especially if it was a child.

"Don't say such a thing!"

"I think I will go and lie down," Posy said. "I'll take the dog with me. Then he won't be under your feet."

As she went, she heard Daff telling George about the way the dog had chased Barry off her seedlings.

In her room, she sat on the bed and stared at the dog. It was exactly as if a dream had come true. She could hardly believe it. She even wondered if she had gotten a concussion and was imagining it all. The dog was padding about the room, sniffing at things. He was making himself at home.

All at once she was overcome by everything. It seemed a lifetime since she had woken up that morning and thought, Hurray, my Great Green Pet Show!

She sank back thankfully and closed her eyes. She would lie and plot the best way to make sure the dog stayed. . . .

Posy opened her eyes. She couldn't for a moment make out what was happening. The curtains were open . . . she wasn't wearing her nightshirt . . . the— the dog! She sat up suddenly and her head buzzed.

The room, she could see at a glance, was empty. The dog had gone. He had strayed into her life out of nowhere, and now he had strayed out again.

Like the bag lady, she thought numbly. (Posy had a real-live bag lady for a friend. She'd met her first in town, then at the village fair.) The world went blurred.

After what seemed a long time, she blew her nose and looked at her watch. Nearly four o'clock! She had missed lunch! She went automatically to the window. That was what she did every morning, to check on the weather.

She looked out. She shut her eyes, counted up to ten, then looked again.

There, under the shade of the may tree, were Daff and George in their deck chairs. The carriage was nearby; there was a tray with tea things. Sitting be-

tween them, his head going from side to side like that of a tennis spectator, to follow as cookies moved from hand to mouth, was the dog. He looked as if he belonged there, like one of the family. As she watched, Daff absently held out a piece of cookie and—the dog sat up on his hind legs!

Even from this distance, Posy could see that her mother was delighted.

As if *she'd* done the trick! Posy thought.

Another cookie was snapped up—and another.

"Oh, hurray!" breathed Posy Bates. "Oh, *brilling!* Pinch me, somebody; I think I must be in heaven!"

Posy Bates and a Snip

"It's all very well for you," Sam said bitterly. "It's not you that gets called Goldilocks."

"Well, no," admitted Posy, whose hair was reddish brown. She would have given anything for yellow hair like his. Sometimes, before she went to sleep, she *willed* it to turn yellow in the night, but it never had. Not yet, anyway.

"Just look at it! Just like a girl's!"

He tugged a lock of it forward, level with his nose, glowered at it, then pushed it back again.

"Trouble is, she wanted me to be a girl. Know why I'm called Sam?"

"Why?"

"Because if I was a girl I was going to've been called Samantha. Samantha—I ask you!"

"I think it's a nice name," she told him. "Better than Posy. And better than Barry," she added. "You should just be thankful the cat got called that instead of you."

"It's a wonder she doesn't make me wear dresses," he went on. "I've got the longest hair of any boy in the whole school."

"It is pretty," said Posy unwisely.

"Pretty? *Pretty?*"

For a moment she thought he was going to sock her one.

"Look, are you coming or not?" she said swiftly, to change the subject. "Mom's given me money for an ice cream. We'll go halves, if you like."

Posy was going to the post office to put up a notice about the dog.

"There's no need," she had protested when Daff told her to. "You've called the police. And he definitely doesn't belong to anyone in the village."

"You never know," Daff told her. "You go and write out a notice. 'Found. Dog, long black hair, white patches. Sits up for cookies'—that kind of thing."

Reluctantly, Posy had done so. She had deliberately made the dog sound as unattractive as possible.

FOUND—STRAY DOG, the notice read. BLACK WITH MATTED-UP FUR. EATS A LOT. NEEDS LOTS OF WALKS AND BARKS A LOT. CALL AT 27 GREEN LANE.

"There's a lot of *lots* in it," Daff had said when

Posy showed it to her. "And what's this about matted-up fur?"

"Well, it was, when we found him. He hadn't been brushed for months—years. Whoever had him didn't deserve him."

"That's true enough," George said. "Looked straight out of the bargain basement. A real bargain basement dog, that!"

And he had started calling the dog that, to Posy's annoyance. Then he decided it was too much of a mouthful, and called him B.B. for short. The funny thing was, the dog seemed to answer to it.

I reckon his first name must've started with a B, Posy thought. So she started calling him Buggins, because it sounded a bit like Bargain Basement, and he'd gotten to know that. Every time she said it, he wagged his tail.

"And you're still B.B.," she had told him. "Not Bargain Basement—Buggins Bates!"

"Are you coming or not?" she asked Sam again.

"I s'pose. . . ." He kicked at a stone, no doubt imagining it to be his mother.

"I'm taking Buggins. Why don't you take your goldfish?"

"For a *walk?* You're crazy, Posy Bates!"

"It'd be a change for him. It must be boring,

swimming around and around in the same place every day."

"Tough," Sam said. "I'm not taking it. That's all I need—long hair *and* taking goldfish for walks!"

Posy called Buggins, who was lying by Fred's baby carriage. She was training him to do this, to get round Daff.

"Good boy!" She clipped on the leash that had been given to her by old Mrs. Kettleborough, who had once had a spaniel called Perkins.

"I bet you can't keep him," Sam said as they set off up the lane. "Bet someone claims him."

"Bet they won't!"

"Will!"

"Won't!"

"You're just jealous," Posy told him, "because all you've got's Barry and the goldfish."

The goldfish was in any case hers, by rights—she had won it at the fair. Then she'd given it to the poor, friendless bag lady for company, and that ungrateful person had given it straight to Sam. Posy had been miffed by this but had not let on to Sam.

She now felt in some obscure way that Buggins was her reward for being unselfish. She had wanted a goldfish badly, at the time. She had given it away, and Buggins, who was worth a million goldfish, had turned up instead. This was the sort of thing that happened in fairy tales, and Posy Bates was inclined to believe in fairy tales.

Posy handed in the notice at the post office and bought a chocolate ice. Once outside, she broke it, rather messily, in two.

"Goldilocks! Hey, Goldilocks!"

"Who's a pretty boy, then?"

"Told you!" Sam said.

Dick Martin and Mary Pye were swinging on the Bootses' gate.

"Come on—come here and I'll put it in pigtails for you!"

"Sissy Post, Sissy Post, we've got hair but he's got the most!"

"Don't take any notice," Posy said. "They only do it to get you mad."

"You shut up, toilets, or I'll pull *your* hair out, by the roots!"

"Temper, temper!"

"C'mon!" said Posy, and started to run. They ran until they were out of earshot.

"I'll cut it myself!" Sam said as they reached Posy's house. "I could do the front, anyhow!"

"I could do it!"

The words were there without Posy having thought them at all. They just came out.

"Oh—would you?"

Posy looked at him. It was not, she knew, a good idea to cut his hair. In fact, it was a terrible idea. Mrs. Post would have a fit. Daff would be told, and Posy's Campaign for Being Good as Gold so that she could keep Buggins would be spoiled. On the other hand, Sam was red and miserable and close to tears and was, after all, her best friend.

"I'll tell you what," she said. "Let's just trim it. Enough not to look like a girl's, but not enough for your mother to notice."

"Have you ever cut hair before?"

Posy hesitated. She had, as a matter of fact, once cut all her dolls' and teddy bears' hair, and gotten a good smacking for it. But that, she told herself, was long ago, when she was young.

"Mom used to be a hairdresser," she told him. "Before she had us."

Perhaps being a good hairdresser ran in families. She hoped so.

"I'll get some scissors," she said. "You wait here. You can be training Buggins to fetch sticks, if you like."

Posy intended to use Daff's special hairdressing scissors, if she could. No one was allowed to use these, as a rule, and they were kept in the top drawer of her dressing table. The trouble was, Daff was up there in her bedroom, tidying out drawers.

"Shall I help?" offered Posy. This would score a point in the Campaign for Being Good as Gold, as well as give her a chance to pinch the scissors.

"No, thank you very much," replied Daff. "If you're in the mood for tidying drawers, your own need a good sorting out."

So Posy went back downstairs to see what she could find. Daff's sewing scissors were very sharp, she knew that, though very small—not much bigger than nail scissors. There were also several other pairs in the kitchen drawer. Posy collected them all and tried them out on a sheet of paper. There was no doubt about it—the sewing scissors were sharpest. She didn't see that it really mattered that they were small. She took those.

In the garden she found Sam and Buggins slumped side by side, tired of throwing and fetching sticks.

"Those look small," said Sam when he saw the scissors.

"They're the sharpest," she told him. "It's very important when you're cutting hair. Blunt scissors just chop at it."

Daff had told her this, plenty of times.

"We'd better go in the shed to do it," she told him. "Where no one can see us."

She got Buggins to lie and stay near Fred's carriage, and the pair of them went into the shed. They stood

uncertainly, looking at each other in the dusty dim-
ness. It certainly did not *smell* like a hairdresser's.
Posy pulled out a wooden beer crate.

"Sit here," she ordered.

Sam obeyed. His beautiful hair gleamed gold, even
in this half-light. Posy swallowed.

The first snip will be the hardest, she told herself.
After that, it'll be easy.

"The main thing is not to get it wonky," Sam said.

"I know that!" she snapped. Her hand was wobbly.
"And if you keep still, it won't be. Now, I'm going to
start this side, then work around the back all the way
to the other."

She took a strand of hair. It felt mysteriously warm
and somehow alive. She dropped it.

"What's up?"

"Nothing. I'm just working out how big a chunk
to cut at a time."

"Big chunks," Sam said. "Then it's bound to be all
the same length."

This sounded true enough. Somewhere inside her
head, Posy thought she could hear Daff saying, "The
art is to cut only a few strands at a time. And to use
the comb. Comb and scissors work together."

"Oh, gubbins!" said Posy. "I've forgotten the comb!"

"Look, are you going to do it or not? If you are,
do it quick!"

Posy hesitated. Then she picked up another strand of hair, a much bigger one this time. It stood to reason that if you cut a big piece, it was bound to turn out all the same length. She took a deep breath. Snip!

As she snipped, the hair seemed to slide away between the blades. She looked down and saw a fat golden curl lying on the dusty boards. She'd done it! And that curl looked exactly like any other snippet she had seen fall when she had gone with Daff to the hairdresser's. (Daff cut the family's hair but drew the line at her own.)

Posy bent and picked up the curl so that she could measure where to cut the next piece. Snip! Then again, and again.

"Can you see my ear?" Sam asked. "Pity there's not a mirror."

"You don't get mirrors in sheds."

Posy stood back and surveyed him.

"Just. You can just see the tip."

"That'll do, then. Just keep going."

Posy did keep going. She was enjoying herself now—the soft slither of the hair, the clean snip of the blades, the tumbling curls. She had no intention of becoming a hairdresser herself when she grew up. She meant to be an Expert on Birds and Beasts. But she did rather feel that hairdressing might run in the family.

Sam himself seemed less nervous now that the cutting was well under way.

"What we could do," he said, "is wait till Mom gets used to it this length, and then cut it a bit more. Then it'd sort of get shorter invisibly."

"She'd think it was shrinking!" Posy giggled. "You could wash it in really hot water, and then go running in and say, 'Look, Mom, my hair's shrunk!'"

She was halfway around now, just above the nape of Sam's neck.

"Posy! Posy!"

They froze. It was Daff's voice, quite close by.

"Posy! Where are you?"

"It's no good!" Posy hissed. "She knows I'm in the garden somewhere. Just stay here and keep quiet!"

She opened the shed door, nipped out, and shut it tightly behind her.

"Oh, there you are!"

"Just giving my spiders a run in the shed, Mom."

This was a very respectable alibi, and at any other time might have been true. After all, Posy did keep two pet spiders in a jam jar in her closet.

"Oh!" Posy's hand flew to her mouth. She had forgotten! How could she be so heartless? "Punch— Judy!"

The spiders had been entered in the Great Green Pet Show, along with Peg the Leg, her stick insect, to whom she had meant to give first prize. That had been two days ago.

"You go and tidy up your room," Daff told her. "I'll be up in a bit with the vacuum cleaner, and it'd be nice to see the carpet."

But Posy was past her, searching for the jam jars and her pets. She had clean forgotten them once Buggins had appeared.

"Oh, no!"

The jars were lying on their sides, knocked over in the rush when the pet show had turned to bedlam, with dogs chasing cats, cats chasing hamsters and mice, and children chasing anything that moved.

"Oh, *no!*"

The jam jars were empty. Punch and Judy and Peg the Leg had gone. She dropped to her knees and started scrabbling in the grass, but she knew it was too late. It was only two days since the pet show, but already it seemed a million years ago.

They were my faithful pets, she told herself dolefully. They trusted me.

"Posy!"

"Oh, can't I do it tomorrow?"

"Now! Come *along*. It'll soon be teatime."

Teatime—when Mrs. Post would be calling for Sam, who was sitting in the shed with his hair half cut. She really had no choice.

"Good-bye, Punch and Judy! Good-bye, Peg the Leg!"

She made for the house.

"Won't be long!" she called loudly, for Sam to hear. "Back in a minute!"

In her room she scooped up socks, puzzles, crayons, scrapbooks, and T-shirts, and pushed them into a drawer.

"I can take these, while I'm at it!" She picked up a comb from the dressing table, and a small mirror. She pushed this under her T-shirt and held it there. Daff would be bound to ask what she wanted it for.

When she went down, Daff was in the kitchen.

"Just off out for a bit!"

"And don't be long. It's nearly teatime."

Back in the shed, Sam was reading an old comic he had found and whistling. This annoyed Posy. After all, it would be she who got into the most trouble if the grown-ups found out. She was doing the cutting.

"I've got a comb," she announced. "And here's a mirror."

She handed it to Sam, then combed the hair she had already cut. Her heart sank. She stepped back, to make sure. There was no doubt about it. Sam's hair, instead of being straight and even, as she had intended, went up and down in zigzags. It looked as if it were scalloped, like the edge of Daff's dressing-table set.

"Oh, you *idiot!*" Sam had the mirror and was turning it this way and that. "It's awful!"

"I'll straighten it up!"

"No!" Sam pushed her away. "That'll make it even shorter, and it'd probably still be wonky. Oh—Mom'll kill me!"

And me, Posy thought. His mom and mine—they'll both kill me.

She looked down at the forlorn little golden scraps of hair on the dusty boards, and wondered if there were any way of sticking them back on again. She shut her eyes and wished for time to go back an hour, to when Sam's hair was long and even.

As they gazed at one another, frozen in misery, Buggins barked furiously outside.

"You stop it! You let my cat alone!"

"Mom!" Sam's face was quite white.

"Is that dog staying? If so, you stop him terrorizing my cat!"

"And you keep your cat on your own side of the fence!"

"Cats don't *have* fences!"

"Well, I *do!* And that cat's over here disturbing my seedlings every five minutes!"

"It's nature! You can't stop nature!"

"You can try," said Daff grimly. "Good boy, Buggins. Good dog!"

"Come on, Barry, come to Mommy! Poor puss, come on!"

"Poor puss, indeed! I'll give him poor puss if I catch him around here again!"

"That dog's right out of control. Sam! Sam!"

Her voice rose to a screech. Sam shut *his* eyes now.

"Sam! I want you back home this minute!"

A short silence. Then the distant bang of a door. Sam and Posy stared at each other, horror-struck. It crossed both their minds, at more or less the same time, that the only thing now was to run away from home.

Without warning the shed door flew open, letting in a flood of light. It was Daff.

"Posy? Have you got Sam here? He'd best—" She stared. She took in the comb, the scissors, the scatter of snipped curls. "What the . . ."

She came in. She looked at Sam, then walked around, inspecting him.

"Well," she said at last, "a fine mess you've made of that, Posy Bates."

Posy gulped.

"I asked her to," Sam said. Posy could have hugged him. "Everyone was calling me Goldilocks."

"I'm not surprised," Daff said. "A boy of your age, and hair that length!"

"I tried to cut it straight!" Posy wailed. "I tried ever so hard. And I used the sharpest scissors!"

Daff looked at the sewing scissors. Then she laughed. Sam and Posy were startled. She seemed to laugh for ages; it was as if she would never stop.

"Her and her cat!" she said at last.

"She'll kill me," Sam said.

"And I'm only half done! What'll we *do?*"

Daff surveyed them again.

"*I'll* cut it," she said. "Come on, the pair of you!"

She turned and went out, and the two followed her into the house, with Buggins at their heels. In the kitchen, she paused.

"Wait here," she ordered, and went upstairs. When she came down, she had her hairdressing scissors and another comb.

"You'd better watch this," she told Posy. "You might do a better job next time."

Then comb and scissors were at work, fast and skillful, and in no time at all the zigzags had vanished and the golden hair was smooth and even all the way around. And it hardly seemed to curl at all.

"There!" Daff stepped back to admire her handi-work. "Take a look!"

Sam got up and peered into the mirror over the mantelpiece.

"It's very nice," he said in a small voice. "Thank you very much, Mrs. Bates. But—but it's shorter!"

"Hair usually is when you cut it," Daff said.

"But she'll notice!" Posy said. "And she'll kill him!"

Daff smiled. She smiled in a slow, triumphant kind of way. "We'll see," she said.

She went out and into the garden and stood at the fence.

"Joan!" she called. "Joan!"

Posy and Sam stood in the doorway watching, breath held.

"Now what?" Mrs. Post came out, still cross and suspicious.

"Sorry about that little tiff just now," Daff said.

"Tongue ran away with me. So I've done you a bit of a favor, to make up."

Mrs. Post was baffled.

"Favor? What kind of favor?"

"Well, as you know, I'm a hairdresser," Daff said. "And I could see your Sam was due for a trim, so I've done it for you. Ridiculous prices they charge, these days."

"Oh, good old Mom!" breathed Posy.

"Sam!" Daff turned and called. "Come and show your mom your nice hair."

Sam gulped and stepped bravely forward with his brand-new hairstyle, well above the tips of his ears now, a shorn Goldilocks.

"There!" said Daff. "Isn't that nice?"

It was Mrs. Post's turn to gulp now. Her Sam had never looked less like a Samantha.

"I'll do it for you regular, if you like," Daff offered.

"Well, it's very kind of you, Daff, but—"

"That's settled, then," said Daff. "Nice world if you can't do a neighbor a good turn once in a while. Off you go, Sam, for your tea. Come along, Posy."

And she went back in, followed by Posy, leaving Mrs. Post thunderstruck. Posy, who was by now in the habit of scoring points, gleefully thought, Mom, a thousand; Ma Post, *zero!*

Posy Bates Cleans Up

"I could do without half terms," Daff was saying. "Though I dare say teachers can do with the rest."

Posy took no notice. Daff said this every half term, more or less.

"*I* don't like half terms either," Pippa said. "Boring. Miss Gisborne's gone to Majorca."

"Very nice," said Daff. "Isn't it time you were off, George? Then I can get these things cleared."

George always took a long time over breakfast. He seemed to space it out to fit in with reading his newspaper.

The phone rang. Posy jumped. The phone had been making her jump ever since Buggins had arrived and Daff had reported him to the police.

Please let it not be the police, she prayed. Twice around the garden shed, once around the sundial, clap your hands five times, shut your eyes, and say the magic word.

This was Posy's secret charm. She couldn't actually *do* it at this moment, but at least she could pretend to inside her head, and at least she could silently say the magic word.

"I never!" she heard Daff say. "What—yesterday? Oh, yes—he's still here."

Posy's heart went bang, bang. *He's still here!* The dog—Buggins! Someone was going to claim him; they'd drive up and bundle him into a car, and he'd be gone forever.

I'll run away, she thought. We'll run away together. I'll be a bag lady—well, a bag girl, anyway.

She and Buggins would wander the wide world together. They'd sleep under drafty bridges and hear the night trains roar over their heads. They'd watch the stars.

"That's a nice thing!"

There was a ping as the receiver went down.

"What's that, Daff?" said George.

"Good thing you hadn't gone," Daff told him. "I need you to drive me over to Kneesall. That was Mrs. Parkins."

"Hurray!"

Daff gave her a sharp look. Posy didn't care. It wasn't the police. Mrs. Parkins lived next door to Gran and took messages for her. Gran didn't have a telephone. This was partly because she said she couldn't afford one, and partly because she didn't believe in telephones.

"There's only bad news ever comes over a telephone," she would tell Posy. "And when you get to my age, you've had enough bad news to last a lifetime."

On this occasion it looked as if it *was* bad news that had come over the telephone. Though not, from Posy's point of view, the worst news in the world.

Gran had had a fall the day before.

"Slipped on the path and fell," Daff said, "and now she's in bed and won't get up."

"Can't?" asked George.

"Can't or won't. You know Mother. Cussed as they come."

Posy was sometimes shocked by the way Daff talked about her own mother. Her father—Posy's granddad—was dead. He had died when Posy was about four, and she couldn't remember much about him. She remembered that he had smelled of tobacco and had given her a lot of sweets. According to Daff he had been a layabout, and good for nothing but throwing darts.

"Anyhow," Daff was saying. "I'll have to get over there and see what's to do. And if need be, I s'pose, bring her back here with us."

"I'll call Mrs. Barnes and tell her I won't be able to start her windows till after lunch," George said. (He was a painter and decorator.)

"Pity I can't get out of *my* work as easy," Daff said. "You can trust her to pick a time when I'm up to my ears. There's half a week's washing, for a start. Get Fred changed, Posy, will you, while I get ready?"

Posy lifted Fred out of his high chair and laid him on the rug. Buggins went over and sniffed and wagged his tail. Fred beamed. It was lucky, Posy thought, that Fred was so often smelly. Dogs liked smells, and it was very important that Buggins and Fred should like each other.

"Gran might be coming," she told Fred as she started on his diaper. "She's the one who pokes you in the tummy and calls you Pesky. She might have a broken bone."

Fred did not seem to be interested in any of this. He kept moving his head to follow Buggins. It occurred to Posy that he probably didn't know what a bone was. If he was going to be a genius, he definitely needed to know about bones.

"The thing is," she began, "everybody's got bones. Mom and Dad and Pippa and me—we've all got bones. They sort of hold us together. If we didn't have them, we'd be all wobbly, like jelly. I expect we'd just crumple to the floor. Goodness knows how many bones we've got—dozens, I should think. I'll look it up and let you know later."

Fred's attention was still wandering.

"Even you've got bones," she told him. She took hold of his arms. They felt amazingly soft and boneless, but she managed to find his elbows, and gave them a squeeze. *These* are bones. They're elbows."

Fred did beam at her now.

"Elbows make your arms bend," she told him. "Otherwise they'd just stick straight out. And here are your knees, and these little teeny ones are your toe bones."

Fred was chortling now. Posy leaned forward and kissed his milky face.

"I *think* you've got bones in your face as well," she went on. "You have in your nose, anyway."

She looked at him doubtfully.

"Your nose doesn't look much as if it's got a bone," she said. "It's too little." She fingered it anxiously. "Anyway, don't worry; I expect it has."

She certainly hoped so. She did not relish the idea of a noseless brother.

"Haven't you got that diaper on yet?"

Daff was back with her coat and handbag.

"Come along, look sharp!"

Daff looked about her at the scattered remains of breakfast and the trail of bricks and toys.

"A fine mess to leave," she said. "And all that washing. I do wish you were more help in the house, Posy."

This remark was very unfair, Posy thought. It seemed to her that she was forever doing jobs.

"What about Pippa?"

"Your sister's got her schoolwork. She's got exams to work for."

Pippa had melted away as soon as she had had breakfast. She always did. And Posy knew for a fact that Pippa would not be slaving away at her schoolwork up in her room. She'd be listening to her favorite group through headphones, so that Daff wouldn't hear, and probably sorting through her collection of earrings. Either that, or doing exercises to make her bottom smaller. (In fact, Pippa said it was her hips, but as far as Posy was concerned, it was her bottom.)

"There you are!" she told Fred, and passed him up to Daff.

"Here! What's that?" Daff was staring at the carpet. "Just look—dog hairs!"

Posy looked. It was undeniable. There were several strands of long black hair that could not have come from anywhere but Buggins's shaggy coat.

"I'll pick them up! There's only a few!"

"The point is, Posy, it's unhygienic," Daff said. "I don't want to see them when I get back."

George picked up the baby carrier. They went out and Posy heard the van start and drive off. She looked at Buggins.

"These," she said severely, pointing to the hairs, "are yours. You've lost one point, leaving them there. The thing is, I'd better work out how to score a few points for you now, or you'll end up at the SPCA."

It was obvious from the way Buggins wagged his tail that he had never heard of the SPCA. Posy sat and pondered. It didn't take long to work out how to score those points.

"You'll have to wait for your walk," she told Buggins. "I'm going to tidy everything up. And when Mom gets back, she'll be tickled pink."

She started picking up the strewn toys.

"Tickled pink," she repeated. "Pickled tink. Tickled pink, pickled tink."

Then she started to clear the breakfast things into the kitchen.

"She'll be happy as Larry. Lappy as Harry. Happy as Larry, lappy as Harry."

By the time she had filled the sink with hot, soapy water, she had thought of another.

"Like a dog with two tails, a tog with two dales. . . ."

She sang her brand-new sayings under her breath as she washed the dishes.

I'd have to do them, anyway, she told herself, so's Pippa will stick up for Buggins.

Once the dishes were clean and put away, Posy turned her attention to the living room.

"Do with a good dust and vacuum," she decided.

It was while she was vacuuming that disaster struck. Posy thought that she had picked everything up off the floor. She was happily pushing the machine under the table to pick up crumbs and muttering, "Dust and vacuum, vust and dacuum," when it gave a terrible sort of scream, as if in pain, and ground to a halt.

"Oh, no!" If she'd busted the vacuum cleaner, bang went her points.

She dropped to her knees and turned the vacuum cleaner over. She saw at once what had happened.

"Oh, it would have to be something of mine!" she wailed.

Before old Mrs. Kettleborough had given her the leash for Buggins, Posy tried to make one by braiding string. And now that string was tangled in the brushes—tangled right around the works, for all she knew. She tugged and pulled, but it was hopeless, she knew that. She sat back on her heels and looked at Buggins, who had crept out of the way and was watching warily.

"I've gone and busted the vacuum!" she told him.

This was calamity with a capital *C*.

"And it would have to be your leash that did it!" she added.

In her mind's eye she could already see George putting Buggins in the back of the van to drive him to the SPCA.

"Oh, no, no!"

She fetched a dustpan and brush and finished the carpet with that. She brushed furiously, her mind spinning.

She had to think of something extra specially marvelous to do for Daff, something that would cancel

52

out the broken vacuum. The trouble was, she couldn't.

Flowers! she thought at last.

She knew that this was not a big enough thing, but it would do for a start. She fetched a jug and a vase, filled them with water, and went out into the garden, followed by Buggins. Sam was on the other side of the fence.

"Are you playing?"

"No. I'm not. Got a lot to do."

A dot to lo, she added silently, because once you'd started doing this, it was hard to stop.

"Shall I help you?"

Posy hesitated. She knew Mrs. Post said that whenever Sam helped he made more trouble than it was worth. On the other hand, she would say this, being his mother. At least if Sam came over she'd have someone to talk to, someone to take her mind off the awful looming prospect of the SPCA.

"All right."

He was there in a flash. Daff said he'd live at their house, given half the chance.

"I'm picking flowers," she told him. "For arrangements."

"That all? Won't take two seconds."

"But I've got to think of something else. Something absolutely total."

She told him about Gran falling and not getting out of bed. She told him about the busted vacuum.

"And I've *got* to think of something to put her in a good mood. She was going on and on about all the work and mess and the washing."

"Washing," repeated Sam. "You could do that."

She stared. The thought had never even crossed her mind. Daff was the only one who ever used the washing machine. It was practically a law of nature.

The sun came up in the morning and the leaves fell off in autumn, and Daff always did the washing.

On the other hand, Posy was thinking, what are laws for but to be broken? And how amazed, how utterly astounded Daff would be if she got home to find the washing done—and perhaps even hanging on the line.

"But—I don't know how to work the machine."

"Easy," Sam told her. "Where is it?"

She led the way in.

"I've seen Mom do it tons of times," Sam said.

"Well, so have I," Posy admitted. "But I didn't exactly notice what she did."

"Simple. Where are the things?"

Posy went up and scooped out the contents of the laundry basket. There were socks, pants, underwear, shirts, towels. There was one particular towel that she knew was brand-new. Daff had bought it in Nottingham, in the market, and had shown it to them. It was a truly horrible color, an almost fluorescent lime green. It seemed odd to Posy that her mother had put a new towel in for washing. She shrugged, and piled it up with the rest. She staggered back down, arms so full she could hardly see where she was going.

"Shove it in," Sam said.

He seemed very sure of himself. It was usually
Posy who gave the orders.

"Now— there should be a little drawer thing, for
the powder. Here it is."

Sure enough, he pulled out a small drawer, and it
was certainly the right place for the powder, because
you could see patches of it still stuck to the bottom.

"Where's the powder?"

Posy opened the cupboard under the sink. There
were two boxes, both already started.

"This one," Sam said. "It says *automatic,* see? If you use the other, there's all foam and it froths everywhere and busts the machine."

Posy shuddered at the narrowness of her escape. She certainly would not have known this. She carefully filled the little drawer with powder, then pushed it back in.

"Now—program." Sam studied the dials, with their numbers and signs. "Not the same as Mom's, not exactly. All I know is that if Mom wants things really clean, she puts them on number one."

"Put it on one, then!"

Posy wanted the washing to be marvelously, fabulously clean. Mega clean. She wanted Daff to shower her with praise.

Sam set the dial, then pressed it. Whoosh! The machine had started.

"Oh, hurray!" Already she could hear the water rushing. "When will it be done?"

"Give it a chance," Sam said. "I dunno. Depends. More than half an hour, anyway."

Posy arranged the flowers and placed the jug on the table, the vase on the mantelpiece. Every now and then she went and peered at the busy, whirling machine.

"Doing that won't make it any quicker," Sam said.

So she locked the back door, left the key in the secret hiding place, and they took Buggins for his walk. She had clean forgotten that Pippa was in the house. They were halfway down the path when there was a rap on the window. Pippa opened it and stuck her head out.

"Where are you going?"

"Walk. I've locked the back door."

Daff said you should always lock the back door if you were upstairs, anyway. She said burglars and murderers nearly always just walked into houses, when people were upstairs.

"Oh, charming. What if there's a fire?"

"You'll have to jump out the window," Posy told her. "Wump out the jindow."

And they went off, laughing. They walked down the lane, over the stile, and into the cow pastures. They threw sticks for Buggins, and every now and then Posy said, "D'you think it'll be done yet?"

When they got back, Posy opened the back door and knew at once by the silence that the machine had finished its work. She had actually done the washing! She could hardly believe it, and Daff certainly wouldn't be able to.

A hundred points! she told herself. A thousand! A million!

Sam went and worked out how to open the machine door, while she fetched the yellow plastic basket Daff used to carry the washing to the line.

The door opened. Sam started to pull the things out. Posy froze. Her heart seemed to stop beating.

"Oh, gubbins! Double gubbins!"

A T-shirt—green. Daff's undies—green and wrinkled. A towel—green and streaky. Fred's undershirts—green and tiny, as if for a doll.

Posy shut her eyes. She wanted to keep them closed forever.

"Oh, no!" she heard Sam say. "Everything's green!"

She kept her eyes shut and stopped breathing.

"It's small as well. The stupid machine's gone and shrunk things!"

"Oh, what'll I do, what'll I do?" Posy wailed.

"Mom'll kill me!"

"Mmm. Might fade, I s'pose," Sam said. "Fade in the sun. Let's hang it up, and then perhaps it'll have faded by the time she gets back."

Posy did not really believe this. And certainly the sun wouldn't stretch Fred's undershirts back to their proper size. But it was her only chance.

They carried the washing out and pegged it on the line. It looked greener than ever out there.

"I think I'd better go home," Sam said nervously when they'd finished.

"Lucky you!" said Posy bitterly.

He went. Posy took a last look at the line of green, wrinkled washing, then went upstairs and climbed into her closet. Buggins stayed outside—she had already tried to coax him to come in, but he wouldn't. She wished Punch and Judy and Peg the Leg were still there, to comfort her. She wished she could disappear.

As it was, all she could do was crouch there, waiting for the sound of the van coming up the drive, and the shriek when Daff saw a line of lime green washing to greet her.

And that was only for starters. Then there was the mangled vacuum cleaner. . . .

Posy Bates and Vanishing Fred

What saved Posy from being killed, and Buggins from being sent straight off to the SPCA, was Gran. There was a lot of shrieking when Daff saw the line of green, shriveled washing. Posy, crouched in her dark closet, pressed her hands over her ears.

Then, when they came into the house, there was more shrieking. Daff had found the mangled vacuum cleaner.

"Posy! Posy!"

She crawled out of the closet and went slowly down. She closed her bedroom door behind her, to keep Buggins in (he had come inside, at last). She did not want there to be any connection in Daff's mind between the botched washing and Buggins.

In the uproar that followed, Gran—who was sitting in the high, winged chair bought specially for her— was Posy's champion from the start.

"The child was only trying to help." If she said that

once, she said it ten times. And, "It's the thought that counts."

To this, Daff replied bitterly that thoughts wouldn't turn her washing white, or unshrink it. George spoke very little, because he was busy with the vacuum cleaner. But it wasn't long before he said, "There we are. Good as new. No harm done."

"You'd better get started making my laundry good as new," Daff told him ungratefully. "Really, Posy— to put that brand-new towel in! Don't you know anything?"

"If you'd taught her, she would," Gran said. "How's she to know things if you don't teach her?"

And so it went on, and on, and on. The only good thing, Posy thought miserably, was that what had happened had absolutely nothing to do with Buggins.

Later, Gran even helped put him in favor, without meaning to.

"What's that?" she demanded when she first saw him.

Posy told her.

"You're not keeping it?" Gran asked Daff.

By now Daff was fed up with Gran. "And why not?" she asked.

"What do you want with a dog? All the feeding they take and all the mess they make."

"Oh, that," said Daff airily. "That's why you'd never let *me* have a dog when I was a kid."

This was news to Posy. Apart from anything else, she found it hard to imagine her mother as a child, though obviously she must have been once.

"Quite useful, a guard dog," Daff went on. "And he keeps the cats off the garden."

"You'll send him back, if you want my advice," Gran said.

"Thank you, Mother," replied Daff sweetly. "I think I'm old enough to make up my own mind whether I want a dog or not."

Things were beginning to look promising for Buggins. Daff started to prepare lunch, and the green washing was dropped. It was never, however, forgotten. It was dragged up endless times, for years. Posy Bates never really heard the last of it.

After lunch, Gran said she wanted to have her afternoon nap in a deck chair in the garden. Posy found the deck chair least likely to collapse and set it up for her in the shade of the apple trees. Fred's carriage was next to her, and Posy and Buggins sat on a rug at her feet.

Soon Gran was asleep and Posy deep in her book. It might have been hours that passed in that cool green shade, or it might have been only minutes, before Posy was startled by barking.

"Sh!" she hissed, glancing nervously at Gran. She looked so peaceful it seemed unlikely that even a pack of wolves would wake her.

"Down! Down! Oh, Posy, quickly—my dress!"

Miss Perlethorpe stood halfway up the path, making little flapping movements at Buggins, who was dancing at her feet.

"He won't hurt!" Posy hurried over. "Just give him a pat. No, Buggins, no!"

"Goodness!" Miss Perlethorpe looked down with distaste. "It's not yours, Posy?"

Posy explained about him, and about the police and the SPCA.

"It's only to be hoped that his real owners come forward," said Miss Perlethorpe. "He seems a very rough sort of dog—not at all suitable."

Posy supposed that Buggins was something of a scalawag compared with Selina, Miss Perlethorpe's white poodle. All the same, she thought it very rude to make personal remarks, especially in Buggins's hearing.

"I have really come to see your mother and father, Posy," Miss Perlethorpe told her. "Are they in?"

"Mom is."

Posy followed her up the path, trying to remember any trouble at school Miss Perlethorpe might have come to complain about. It was lucky, she thought, that Daff had snatched the lime green washing off the line. Miss Perlethorpe would have had plenty to say about that.

It turned out that Miss Perlethorpe, who was forever setting projects for her pupils, now had one of her own. She was collecting what she called "interesting old sayings" from people in the village. These were in danger of disappearing, she told Daff.

"I blame it on the television," she said. "Nobody speaks picturesquely these days. Do you have any little words or phrases that you remember, Mrs. Bates?"

"None that I can think of just at the moment," said Daff unhelpfully. "I've got a lot on my mind."

"You know the sort of thing. For instance, the word *hoppit*. Several people have told me that. It means messy, in a muddle, scruffy. . . ." Her eyes rested on Buggins as she spoke. "Such a wonderful word! I had never heard it before today—but then, of course, I come from the south."

"Don't they have sayings down there, then?" inquired Daff.

"Of course, it's the older generation who remember most," Miss Perlethorpe said.

"Ah." Daff smiled. "In that case, Miss Perlethorpe, I think you'd better have a word with *her*."

She pointed to the peacefully slumbering Gran.

"I wouldn't wake her, mind," Daff said. "Or you might hear a quaint old saying you hadn't bargained for."

Miss Perlethorpe was enchanted. "Oh, a *real* old inhabitant!"

"I'll tell Gran when she wakes, if you like," Posy offered.

"Oh, would you? Thank you, Posy dear."

Off she loped, all pearls and bangles. The Bateses watched her go.

"I dare say *her* first name isn't Tracey," observed Daff, and shut the door.

Posy wandered back to the shade. She hoped Gran
would remember some old sayings. For one thing,
she would be quite interested in them herself, and
for another, it would help get her into Pearly's good
books.

She looked at her own book. That had been good,
to start with, but now it had tailed off. Some books
did that. She glanced at the last couple of pages, just
to make sure it actually ended the way she thought
it would, then shut it.

She looked about her. Gran was snoozing. Fred was fast asleep in his baby carrier. The whole world, it seemed, was sleeping. Posy was seized by a kind of desperation, a fierce wish that something would happen—anything! It was a feeling she usually got on Sunday afternoons.

What if Buggins could do something really wonderful, like Lassie! she thought. Something that'd make sure he stayed with us forever and ever!

But Buggins, too, had his head down and his eyes shut. He did not look at all like a dog who was about to perform an amazing feat. The only trick he could do, so far as they knew, was sit up for cookies.

What would be absolutely total, she thought, would be if someone came and kidnapped Fred, and Buggins found him.

That would be perfect. The trouble was that there was no one in sight, let alone a kidnapper.

"Posy!"

It was Sam Post, peering through the gap in the hedge. She went over.

"Was she mad?"

"What do you think? Hopping mad. Mopping had!"

He giggled, and she frowned at him.

"It's not funny. What if she won't let me keep Buggins?"

"*He* didn't do it."

"Not the point," Posy told him. "I was just thinking how brilliant it'd be if a kidnapper came and took Fred, and then Buggins saved him."

"Fat chance," said Sam.

Posy looked at him. She pondered. An idea floated effortlessly into her head.

"Of course, he wouldn't *really* have to be kidnapped," she said thoughtfully. "Just for Mom to think he had been. I reckon you owe me a favor. I got your hair cut, and it was you said you knew how to use the washing machine."

"What?" he demanded.

"Look," said Posy, "all you've got to do is take the baby carrier and hide it. You needn't take it far—just into the field. Then Buggins can sniff it out and he'll be a hero!"

"But how d'you know he *will* sniff it out?"

"Oh, he'll be with me, and I'll know where it is!" Posy was triumphant. "Put him by the hedge, under the second tree down."

Sam looked dubious.

"What if he yells?"

"He won't. He won't wake up for ages yet."

"But what if your mother sees me?"

"She won't. And if she does, we'll just say Fred woke up and we were rocking him to get him to sleep again."

Still he hesitated.

"You daren't!"

"Dare!"

"Daren't!"

"Dare! Right, I will then!"

He crawled through the hedge and marched past the slumbering Gran and lifted the baby carrier. Buggins opened one eye, then closed it again.

"Go over the fence!" Posy hissed. "Straight into the field. Then no one'll see you."

There was a stile from the Bateses' garden into the meadow, and between them they hauled the baby carrier over it.

"I'm going back, to pretend to be asleep," she told him. "Remember—second tree down!"

She sped back under the apple boughs and threw herself down onto the rug and shut her eyes. All she had to do now was wait. She pictured the scene— the discovery that the baby carrier had gone, Daff shrieking, then she and Buggins bounding into the field.

I'll keep yelling, "Find, Buggins! Find!" Then everyone'll think he did it!

She pictured the praise and patting, Daff saying over and over again, "Oh, Buggins, you clever dog!"

But even as she did so, Posy Bates had an uneasy feeling that her plan was not quite perfect. There was

something wrong, something that didn't fit. She pictured then what would happen if a *real* kidnapper came stealing up, past the three sleeping figures—herself, Gran, Buggins.

Of course! Buggins was meant to be a guard dog! He would've woken, and barked and growled and chased the kidnapper off. She lay frozen in horror. What had she done?

I'll have to get him back, she thought. Quick!

"Dear, oh, dear!" It was Gran, waking.

It was too late.

"Posy?" A pause. "Bless her!"

Posy mumbled and stirred and made a great show of waking up.

"What? Oh! I must've fallen asleep."

"We need our sleep, old and young alike," said Gran placidly.

Would she turn her head to check that Fred, too, was sleeping? Posy held her breath. She didn't. As a matter of fact, Gran took very little notice of Fred. Daff would sometimes remark jealously on this, and Gran would reply that he didn't have much to say for himself.

"He might be more interesting when he says something," she would say.

Posy toyed with the idea of drawing attention to the missing carrier herself, but decided it might look suspicious. She would simply have to hope that Gran would notice before Daff did. Then she and Buggins could go through the pantomime of finding Fred, and Daff need never know about it. Gran wouldn't tell, Posy knew, not if she begged her not to. She always took Posy's side against Daff.

"Fred sleeps a lot," she said hopefully.

Gran did not so much as turn her head. "Ah. Well. He might be a bit more interesting when he's got something to say."

"He's all bawl and bottle," Posy agreed. "Hey,

Gran—did you know I'd made an invention? I invented the bottle sockle!"

And she told Gran about it, and Gran said how clever she was and that she was surprised Daff hadn't thought of it herself.

"Mom calls it a bottle cozy, but I call it a bottle sockle."

"Bottle sockle," repeated Gran. "Good."

And this reminded Posy of Miss Perlethorpe and her collection of old sayings, and she told Gran about that, too.

"I bet you know hundreds," she said.

"Ay, well, one or two. . . . Let's see. . . . Oh . . . things *my* mother'd say when I was little. . . ."

"Like what?"

Gran thought. She frowned a little, as she always did.

"Mmm. Main ones I can think of have to do with being hungry. Folk were hungry, you know, in those days."

"Oh, I get hungry," Posy assured her. "In fact, I'm nearly always hungry."

"Never gone without a meal, though, because there was nothing in the house."

Posy reflected. This was true.

"You know what my mom'd say to us, if we asked her what was for dinner, and she'd nothing to give us?"

"What?"

"Two jumps at the cupboard door!"

"What?"

"Two jumps at the cupboard door!"

"What's that mean?"

"I know what it meant to *us*," said Gran grimly. "It meant nothing. It meant a bit of crust, at most, and not even a spread of margarine."

"How terrible!" Posy was aghast.

"And you know what else she'd say?"

"What?"

"Bread and pull it!"

"Pullet?" echoed Posy. "That's chicken, isn't it? You mean bread and chicken?"

"I said pull it and I meant pull it," Gran told her. "Just plain bread. That was a kind of a joke, I suppose."

Posy could see nothing funny whatsoever in only having dry bread for dinner, and said so.

"I bet that's all the bag lady gets sometimes," she said.

"The who?"

"Oh, nothing."

Posy Bates did not talk about the bag lady. She thought of her as somehow magical, and had a superstitious fear that if she were talked about, she might disappear forever.

"Those are good sayings, Gran. You definitely ought to tell them to old Pearly. Can you think of any more?"

There was a long silence.

"Anything to do with babies?" prompted Posy hopefully. When, oh, when, would Gran turn her head and notice that the carrier was missing?

"Oh, *babies*," said Gran dismissively. She did not turn her head. Posy turned hers, though, just in time to see Sam sneaking back from the lane into his own garden. She groaned. It was done now. He had left the peacefully snoozing Fred under the second tree down. She was done for now.

As she looked, Sam glanced over and, catching his eye, she waved. It struck her that perhaps there was a glimmer of hope. Perhaps Sam could hurry back and fetch Fred before anyone noticed he was missing.

She made a face, mouthed the words, "Fetch him back!" and pointed desperately in the direction of the meadow. Sam stood and stared blankly back at her. Then he stuck up his thumb and grinned. He was telling her, "Mission accomplished!"

She grimaced and mouthed and pointed, and all he did was stand and grin.

"What's going on?" demanded Gran, who was not blind, even if she couldn't spot a missing baby right under her nose.

"Got to tell Sam something!"

She jumped up and sped over the hedge.

"Quick! Fetch him back!"

"What? Who? Fred?"

"Yes. Quick. Fetch him back!"

"But I've only just—"

"Quick!" She spat out the word.

He shrugged. "All right. You're crazy, Posy Bates."

He sauntered back down the path. He was not going to hurry, she could see that. Every now and then he got fed up with being ordered about.

"Please!" she called after him.

He shrugged again but did not quicken his pace. She just wished his hair would grow an inch in a minute. She hesitated, uncertain whether to go back to her rug or into the house, where she could try to sidetrack Daff.

The latter, she decided. If worse came to worst, she could clutch her head and pretend to get dizzy. Daff would then think that she had *delayed* delayed concussion, and by the time she'd finished fussing, Fred would be safely back under the apple trees.

When she went in, the house seemed very quiet. There was no sign of Daff in the kitchen. She gently pushed open the door of the living room and saw that Daff was dozing in an armchair. She was just thanking her lucky stars when she put her foot on one of Fred's trucks.

She screamed and threw up her arms, but could not save herself, and was down.

"Posy! *Posy?*"

"'S all right, Mom. Go back to sleep."

"Gracious, I must've dropped off. What are you doing?"

"Just tripped." Posy scrambled up. "Over one of—" She stopped in midsentence. It would be fatal to mention Fred.

"Is that the time?" Daff was getting up herself now, cross as she always was if woken suddenly.

I've made things go from bad to worse, thought Posy.

To her relief, Daff went out and up the stairs. Posy looked out of the window. There, to her amazement, was Sam, running, positively running up the path, and—without the baby carrier!

"Oh, gubbins!"

Posy shut her eyes. Fred had been kidnapped, really kidnapped. She knew it. She also knew that shutting her eyes would not help—not this time. She ran to the door and flung it open. Sam's face was scarlet; he was gasping.

"He's gone! Oh, Posy, he's gone!"

They stared at each other, horror-struck.

"He can't be!" Posy wailed.

Little rosy Fred who was all bawl and bottle, Fred who was going to be a genius—gone forever! By now she had forgotten about Daff and her fury, even forgotten about Buggins and the SPCA. All she could think about was Fred, with a beam at one end and an everlasting wet bottom at the other.

They ran out.

"Where'll we start looking?"

"Oh—what if someone's taken him off in a car!"

They raced down the drive and onto the road, and Posy's mind was in a black whirl. If Fred was gone, *really* gone, it would be the end of the world. It was unimaginable that she might never set eyes on him again, never again pull his wet thumb from his mouth or tell him her secrets.

Whatever they had expected to see, it was not this.

Tottering toward them, lugging Fred's baby carrier, was Pippa.

"Wheeeee!" Posy felt a surge of joy so enormous that she felt as if she might take off and fly, and at the same moment she burst into tears.

She saw only a blur when Pippa dropped the carrier at her feet.

"Here—*you* carry it now. And what on earth did you think you were doing, crazy little kid?"

"I—thought he'd b-been stolen!" Posy sobbed.

"And serve you right if he had been," said Pippa heartlessly. "If I hadn't found him, anyone might've."

"But he was *gone!*" Sam said.

"I hid with him behind the tree, didn't I? To see what was going on. *I* saw you. Your face, when you thought he was gone!"

"Rat!" Sam told her. "Toilet!"

"I wouldn't go calling *me* names," Pippa said. "I could tell *your* mom about this, as well as ours."

"Oh, don't, don't!" Posy pleaded.

Pippa watched as Posy wiped her eyes on her sleeve.

"*How* long was it you were going to do my share of washing the dishes? Well . . . let's say a month, now."

"Oh, yes, yes!"

"And you promise never to go losing him again?"

"Oh, I promise, I do! Oh, Fred!"

She bent to the carrier and lifted him out, warm and drowsy. She had glimpsed for a terrifying moment the huge, yawning hole that would be left without him.

"Sorry, sorry," she murmured into his damp neck.

Posy Bates spent quite a lot of her time having to say sorry, but this was probably the first time in her life she'd meant it. She was really and truly, absolutely totally—sorry.

Posy Bates
Goes Camping

"Well, I just think she's *mean*," said Posy. "When you go camping you're a sort of gypsy, and gypsies have dogs."

That weekend the Brownies were going camping. Posy had wanted to take Buggins. She had begged Miss Perlethorpe.

"Please, oh, please! He'd be a guard dog. And he could catch rabbits for a stew."

She did not really mean this. She could hardly bear to think of a dead rabbit, let alone a skinned one.

"Absolutely not, Posy," Miss Perlethorpe had told her. "I shall not even be taking Selina."

Fat lot of use she'd be even if you did! said Posy—to herself.

Selina was a white poodle with silly frills and a sillier yap.

If Posy had hoped that her family would sympathize, she was disappointed.

"I don't suppose Miss Perlethorpe wants that great thing under her feet all day any more than I do," Daff said.

"I'll give him his walk," George offered.

"Oh, thanks, Dad. But don't—don't let him off his leash, will you?"

Posy was worried that Buggins might run off. After all, he was a stray. For all she knew, once dogs started straying, they kept right on. She was also worried that Buggins might annoy Daff, and end up at the SPCA. On Saturday morning, before she set off, she gave him a good talking to.

"Make sure you chase Barry if he comes around. And don't drop hairs anywhere and don't get under Mom's feet. And if you get the chance, sit up and beg. Mom thinks that's really sweet."

It was hard to tell whether Buggins was taking this in or not.

"I'll only be gone one night," she finished. "So don't think you've got to go straying."

Then she went out to say good-bye to Fred.

"Pity you can't come camping," she told him. "It's brilling in a tent, specially when it rains. Still, I s'pose your carrier's a bit like a tent, in a way. I bet you like to hear the rain pattering on it, don't you?"

Fred gazed back at her, giving nothing away.

"The best part's bacon and eggs on a Primus stove,"

she told him. "And the campfire. You're meant to light it by rubbing sticks together, but old Pearly cheats and uses matches. I won't tell you about matches, because you're too young. Dangerous, fire is. Remind me to show you a box of matches sometime. Then you'll know not to play with them."

Fred closed his eyes. Posy leaned over and kissed him.

"Bye, Freddles. Bye, Fab Fred!"

There were eight Brownies going camping. They were not traveling far—only a few miles—but Posy knew that as soon as they were there, it would be like another world. She had once tried to figure out why, and decided it was to do with smells, mostly. Grass, dew, woodsmoke, Primus stove, wet canvas, frying bacon.

Wish someone'd make *that* into a perfume with matching talc, she thought. I'd ask for it every birthday and every Christmas.

She spent some time wondering what would be a good name for this perfume. "Camping" was rather boring, she decided, and "Primus and Bacon" would perhaps look out of place on a dressing table or in the bathroom, however prettily packaged. "Dawn" sounded plain soppy, and so did "Dew." In any case, none of these names included everything. The only possible name, she finally concluded, would be

"Grass Dew Woodsmoke Primus Stove Wet Canvas and Frying Bacon."

"*I'll* invent it when I grow up," she promised herself. (This meant adding another entry to a whole long list of things she was going to do when she grew up, including going to the moon, bleaching her hair, and, of course, being an Expert on Birds and Beasts and Especially Insects.)

Caroline Boot's father and George were helping take the Brownies and their equipment.

"Think you were going for a month!" observed George, as the trunk filled with sleeping bags, tents, pots, and pans.

"Now, are you sure you checked off every single item on your list?" said Miss Perlethorpe. "And then checked again?"

"Yes, Miss Perlethorpe," the Brownies chorused, and the little convoy moved off.

Ten minutes later they were standing in their field and feeling curiously abandoned, because the tents weren't up yet.

Must be how that bag lady feels, Posy thought. She hasn't got a tent.

"*This* year," said Miss Perlethorpe, "I hope that no one has forgotten anything. Such as tent poles."

This with a look at Posy, who last year had indeed forgotten the tent poles.

"Is it nearly lunchtime?" asked Vicky Wright.

"No, it is not," replied Miss Perlethorpe, "as you very well know. We shall have meals only at proper times. You are overweight, Vicky, and the last person who should be snacking."

"Oh, the rude *thing!*" hissed Posy indignantly. "You're not supposed to make personal remarks. You'd think a Brown Owl'd know that!"

The minute she had a chance, she whispered to Vicky, "She's a rude thing saying that about you, and you're not overweight. If she says it again, tell her she's got a long nose. Tell her she's got a nose like Pinocchio when he'd told about twenty lies!"

They both fell about giggling, and got a stern look from down Miss Perlethorpe's long nose.

Once the tents were up, the field began to look more like home. There were two big tents and one small—for Brown Owl. Posy was sharing with Vicky Wright, Caroline Boot, and Emma Hawksworth. They had already plotted to bring extra food for a midnight feast, and were going to tell ghost stories while they ate it.

Once the tents were up and everything stowed in place, Miss Perlethorpe announced lunch. This was packed sandwiches.

"We shall not make the campfire until this evening," she said. "This afternoon we shall all gather sticks for it. And then—" she paused—"we shall practice our tracking!"

The Brownies cheered, as they always did. Whenever they came camping, the ritual was always the same. Miss Perlethorpe would disappear into the woods and tell the Brownies that they were to follow, in pairs, at ten-minute intervals. She laid a careful trail of sticks and pebbles and arrows for them to follow. Yet this particular pack of Brownies never seemed to get any better at tracking; she couldn't work out the reason why.

This, quite simply, was because the Brownies had no intention of finding her. They just switched her arrows in different directions, and tracked one another instead. All the signs became gloriously confused, and the result was a long, exciting romp in the woods, with Brownies all over the place, hiding behind trees and pouncing out on one another. It ended, in fact, with everyone being what Miss Perlethorpe called "extremely silly."

The Brownies *liked* being extremely silly. It was what they came camping for in the first place, mostly.

At three o'clock, with the campfire stacked and ready for lighting, they stood and watched their leader disappear among the trees. She had her Brownie handbook under her arm, and would spend the rest of the afternoon in a bush, reading it and waiting vainly to be found.

The Brownies drew straws to decide what order they should set off in. Posy and Caroline Boot were to be last.

"Good!" said Posy. It was the best to be last, because by then the track had become hopelessly muddled and anything could happen. On this occasion it did.

She and Caroline waited their ten minutes, then set off into the woods. The first sign they found seemed to be pointing in two directions at once—a kind of double-headed arrow.

"Eeeny, meeny, miney, mo!" said Posy, giggling. This was a promising start.

They chose the left-hand fork, and were just straightening up after finding the next marker when they were startled to see Vicky Wright and Emma Hawksworth, who had set off first. They were running, crashing through the undergrowth and leaping over fallen trees as if their lives depended on it.

"Is Pearly after them?" Caroline wondered.

The pair panted to a halt. They were so out of breath that they were talking in puffs. It seemed that they had met an old woman.

"Down . . . by the stream!" panted Vicky.

"A witch!" said Emma. "I'm sure she was!"

"All hunched up, with horrible, dirty fingers . . ."

"And she never said a word. . . ."

"Not a single word!"

"Just glared at us, with these awful black eyes . . ."

"Putting a spell on us!"

Posy and Caroline, who had not seen this fearful vision, were not convinced.

"Just an ordinary old lady, I expect," said Caroline. "Did she have a pointed hat?"

"Or a black cat?" inquired Posy.

It appeared that the old lady had been wearing a woolly hat and mitts, so was obviously a witch in disguise. The main reason why they knew she was a witch was the fact she had not said a single word, but just stared.

Bells were ringing in Posy Bates's head. Woolly hat and mitts . . . dirty fingers . . . black eyes . . . could it possibly . . . ?

"Did she have any luggage?" she asked.

"Oooh, yes," said Caroline. "Any suitcases full of frogs' legs and toadstools?"

"Shut up!" said Posy. "Did she?"

"Well . . . only these bags. . . ."

"Carrier bags, sort of. . . ."

Oh, *brilling!* said Posy Bates to herself. Oh, amazing—it *is* her!

"Anyway, I'm not going back in there," said Emma. "I'm going to hide in the tent till Pearly gets back."

"Well, I'm going to have a look!" said Posy.

"And me," said Caroline.

Posy paused. The bag lady was *hers*.

"Always wanted to meet a witch," she said.

Caroline hesitated.

"You don't really believe . . . ?"

"Oh, yes, I do," said Posy. "I should think she's a witch, all right. Used to be full of witches, this wood did, in the olden days. Witchy Wood, it used to be called."

Still Caroline hesitated.

"People used to go in here and never be seen again," went on Posy, laying it on with a trowel now. "Especially children. And specially *girls*."

"Ooooh—don't!" Emma and Vicky shrieked and ran off. Caroline followed them.

"You're crazy, Posy Bates!" she yelled over her shoulder.

Posy smiled. She knew the path that led to the stream. Somewhere deep in the woods were four Brownies and Miss Perlethorpe, all waiting to be found. As she went, she kicked at all the twiggy arrows and pebbles. Now nobody could find *anybody,* she thought with satisfaction.

Except me. And I'm going to find that bag lady or bust!

Sure enough, it was the bag lady and not a witch who sat by the stream. She just sat. She was not reading a book or washing her feet or fishing for minnows. She just sat.

Not even waiting for someone to find her, thought

Posy. Again she was seized with unbearable sadness that anyone should be so alone in the world.

"Bag lady!" she called softly. "It's me. Posy."

The old woman turned her head. She did not speak. She just looked, so long and hard that it was easy to see why the others had taken her for a witch. If Posy had not already met her in the Victoria Center, and at the fair, she might have thought so herself.

The bag lady certainly did not go in for conversation. She hardly ever spoke unless spoken to, and not always then. Posy thought that perhaps her powers of speech had gone rusty, with no one to talk to, and all those wet and windy nights and days traipsing the world.

"We're camping," Posy told her. "Are you?"

It was a silly question. She knew that the minute it was out. The bag lady's life was one long camping, rain or shine.

" 'Course, you're used to camping," Posy said. "A real camper, you are. Bet you haven't even got a tent. Bet you haven't even got a sleeping bag. Bet you just lie down and sleep under the stars."

Still the old lady said nothing.

"Wish *I* could," Posy went on. "I did suggest it, but old Pearly—that's our Brown Owl—she's a real fusspot. Makes us all have sleeping bags and tents. Said we'd all get pneumonia."

There was a long silence, broken only by the running of water over stones. Posy was just going to start another topic of conversation when the bag lady spoke.

"I've had the pneumonia," she said.

"Oh, dear!"

"Nearly died of it. *And* I've got the rheumatics."

"How awful! Old Mrs. Kettleborough gets that. But she's got a copper bracelet. Have you?"

The bag lady was shaking her head. "No tent. No sleeping bag. No copper bracelet."

The bag lady was gazing mournfully down into the

water. Posy desperately wanted to do something to help. She knew for a fact that it was no use asking the bag lady if she'd like to share their tent. Miss Perlethorpe would throw a fit.

Though it would only be Lending a Hand, thought Posy. Doing a Good Deed.

She racked her brains to think of a Good Deed she could do now, right away, to help the rheumaticky old bag lady.

"And I know!"

The bag lady looked at her.

"Wait here!"

Posy sped back through the wood the way she had come. When she reached it, the camp was deserted. She suspected that her tent mates had gone into the nearby village for ice cream. They quite often did on these occasions, when they were sure that Brown Owl was safely stewing in her own juice, waiting to be tracked down.

She dived into the tent, snatched up her Good Deed, and tore back into the wood. The bag lady was still there, sitting motionless, exactly as Posy had left her.

"I'm back!"

The bag lady seemed to have gone into a dream again.

"And I've got something for you!"

The bag lady did turn then. "Food!" she said.

"Oh, gubbins!" How could she have forgotten that the bag lady was always hungry, with a rumbling belly? "I could bring you some later!"

She didn't see how, with Miss Perlethorpe owling about, but she'd find a way somehow.

"Now—look, I've brought you this!"

The old lady stared suspiciously at the rolled-up green bundle.

"It's a sleeping bag. Look!"

Posy untied the strings and rolled out the bag, with its deep quilted ridges.

"Snug as a bug in a rug," she said encouragingly, remembering what Daff had said when she brought it home and Posy had first climbed into it. It was true. There was something marvelously enfolding and comforting about the bag. For the first week after she had it, Posy had insisted on sleeping in it. She would even now, if Daff would let her.

But, "It's unhygienic," Daff had said. "You sleep in a proper bed, Posy, as nature intended."

Posy was going to miss that sleeping bag. She was also going to have a hard job explaining where it had gone. At this moment none of that mattered. All that mattered was that the poor bag lady should know what it meant to sleep snug as a bug in a rug.

"It's really light," Posy told her. "In the morning

just roll it up how it was, and you carry it easy as winking."

The bag lady was obviously interested. She stood up. She unfolded slowly, rustily. Out came a grimy, mitted hand. She turned the bag this way and that. Then she lifted it and pulled it down over her head, as if it were a particularly tall tea cozy.

"No!" cried Posy. "Not like that!"

The bag lady, blinded, waved her arms and tottered wildly. Muffled snorts came from the thick folds. Posy tugged at the bag and it fell off. The bag lady's woolly hat was all awry, her face flushed, her eyes wild and panic-stricken. She bent and snatched up her own shabby bags and started to move off, quite fast.

"No! Don't go! Look—I'll show you! You did it the wrong way around. You put your *feet* in first!"

But the bag lady kept moving, deaf and obstinate. Posy caught up with her, the sleeping bag still trailing.

"Don't go! If you stay, I'll fetch you some food later."

The old lady stopped.

"Go away!" she said. "You're bothering me."

She said it very distinctly, and looking straight ahead. Then she went on.

Posy stood and watched her go, plodding steadily, outlandish among the green undergrowth. When she was out of sight, Posy hauled up the sleeping bag and heaved a deep sigh.

"Oh, *gubbins!*" she said. "You messed *that* up, Posy Bates."

She tramped back to the camp, mad at herself, mad at the whole world. She was particularly mad at Miss Perlethorpe and the rest of the Brownies.

If *she* can't sleep snug as a bug, neither will they! she thought fiercely.

And Posy Bates spoiled everyone's sleep that night, good and proper. When lights were out and Brown Owl safely zipped into her small tent, all the Brownies crowded into one large tent and the secret feast began.

Now it was really dark. Owls hooted and there were rustlings from the nearby wood.

"Tell us a story, Posy!" whispered the others, as they always did.

So Posy did. She told them the story of an old witch—one that two of them had already seen for themselves, that very day.

"Ooooooh!" they quavered, and "Sh—what was that?" and "Oooh, don't!"

But Posy did. She went relentlessly on and on and at the very end shrieked, "Look out—she's there!"

And the Brownies went into hysterics. They screamed and wailed and clutched one another in the darkness. The tent rocked and pitched.

Then Miss Perlethorpe was there, her lamp flashing.

"Silence!" she screeched.

But the Brownies would not be silent. By now Mary Pye and Vicky Wright were sobbing in earnest.

"We want to go home! We want to go home!"

The pandemonium went on and on. It went on even after Brown Owl had pinpointed Posy as the culprit.

"I never heard such rubbish!" she said. "Witch, indeed! Go to sleep this minute!"

At the thought of being fast asleep when that witch came prowling out of the wood, the Brownies set up afresh. If there had only been four of them, Miss Perlethorpe would certainly have bundled them into her car and driven straight home. But there were eight.

And so they had to stick it out till dawn. Some of the Brownies managed to snatch a few hours' sleep, here and there. The only one who didn't get a single wink was their Brown Owl, because at any given time at least one Brownie was awake, and checking up on her. (She had rashly promised that *she* would make sure no witch came creeping up.)

The one who slept soundest of all was Posy Bates herself. But even *her* dreams were haunted—not by a witch, but by a solitary bag lady, out there somewhere in the wood, without so much as a sleeping bag.

Posy Bates and the Homeless

Buggins had been with the Bateses for a whole month now—well, three weeks and six days. Posy was marking off the days on her calendar. Each night she drew a careful green ring around the date. One more day had passed without Buggins's owner turning up to claim him, or Daff packing him off to the SPCA.

"On the very last day I'll put a big *red* ring," she told Buggins. "And we'll have a celebration. Sam and me'll have chocolate cookies and lemonade, and I'll get you billions of bones."

Buggins wagged his tail. He was in every way a far more satisfactory pet than a spider or a stick insect. Just as Posy believed that Fred understood every word she said, so she believed that Buggins did, too. She was not training him to be a genius, as she was Fred, but she gave him plenty of lectures; on behavior, mostly.

This particular Friday, Posy had woken up and

known immediately that it was Friday. It was always a brilliant yellow day, sunshiny whatever the weather. Only a few more hours of school, then Brownies (which she enjoyed despite Miss Perlethorpe's being Brown Owl), and then the whole weekend ahead. But beyond the usual Friday glow, Posy Bates felt in her bones that today would be special, that an adventure was in store. It was all the more important, therefore, that it should not be spoiled.

Every day before leaving for school, she gave Buggins a lecture about how he should behave in her absence. Today, this was longer than usual.

"Now, I want you to remember all the things I've told you," she said. "Number one, don't get under Mom's feet. If you see her feet coming, dodge from under them."

Buggins watched her, head cocked.

"Number two, guard Fred. If anyone comes near his carrier, give a good growl and bark. Number three, try not to let any of your hairs drop out. I know it's not easy—in fact, I can't quite think how you *can* stop them—but try, anyway. Hold your breath or something."

Buggins was still watching her. It was one of the things she loved, the way he watched her face when she was talking, just like Fred did. Nobody else in the world ever gazed at her like that, for minutes on end. All most people ever did was glance at her.

"Those are the main things," she went on. "And you know about not going onto the road. Oh—and Mom's seedlings. If you see Barry, chase him off, and make sure you bark a lot, so's Mom notices. Oooh, and Buggins, it's going to be an absolutely total day today, I know it is!"

She ran off down the path and along the sunlit lane with its wet nettles and whistling birds.

Posy did not have to wait long before she knew for certain that today *was* special. In assembly, Miss Perlethorpe talked about the homeless.

"It is a terrible, terrible thing to have no home to go to," she said.

"Like tramps, you mean," said Caroline Boot.

"Not necessarily tramps," Miss Perlethorpe told her. "All kinds of people—people like you and me. And even children."

Like my bag lady, Posy was thinking. Wandering the wide world alone and always hungry. She wondered where the bag lady was now, and when she would see her again.

". . . a really big effort," Miss Perlethorpe was saying. "Everyone has things at home that are not really needed. And every kind of thing will help. Clothes, bits of furniture, old carpets, perhaps, and bedding. Lots and lots of that—sheets and blankets and pillows. I want every one of you to ask when you get home from school today. Tell your parents what I have just told you."

"There's been a dirty old woman hanging around here, Miss," said Dick Martin. "I reckon she's a tramp."

"I don't think I like that word, Dick," said Miss Perlethorpe. "I expect you'd be dirty if you had no home and no bathroom. If it comes to that, I've seen you looking dirty more than once. And I think *you* have a bathroom at home."

The school tittered.

"Have you seen her lately?" Posy asked Dick at recess. "That dirty old woman?"

Dick shrugged. "On and off," he said. "My ma's seen her as well. Says I'm not to talk to her, and she ought to be put away."

"Then your mother's a silly old bat," said Posy sweetly, and walked away.

Was the bag lady still around, circling Little Paxton? Was she picking through garbage cans in search of food, sleeping under hedges with a bag for a pillow? She conjured up a picture of her, with her bird's-nest hair and cocoon of old clothes, her fingers sticking out from her mitts.

As long as I've got the magic bobbin, I'm bound to see her again, Posy thought. (The bag lady had given her an empty cotton reel on their first meeting in the Victoria Center. She had called it "a magic bobbin," and Posy was sure it was.)

It got me that goldfish, and for all I know it got me Buggins, too.

Miss Perlethorpe told the school that the Brownies would actually collect and sort the donations for the homeless.

"It will be our Good Deed," she said. "Though naturally we shall be grateful if fathers help with the heavier items."

"Have we got any spare things for the homeless?" Posy asked Daff when she got home from school.

"*You'll* be homeless if you don't get that room of yours tidied," Daff said. "What sort of things?"

Posy told her. "In Nottingham they've got houses and hostels and things," she explained. "So they need stuff like furniture. And curtains and lamps and cushions and things to make it cozy. And bedding; Pearly says lots and lots of bedding."

"I s'pose I might dig something out," Daff said. "Get rid of some of the clutter."

"I expect you're grateful you're not a bag lady," Posy said.

"You what?" Daff stared, then laughed. "The very idea! Bag lady, indeed!"

"If you knew of a bag lady who had to sleep under bridges, would you ask her in?" Posy asked.

"No, I would not. I've enough on my plate as it is, thank you, and the place always topsy-turvy and littered up—you might as well be living in a henhouse!"

Posy stared. A marvelous thought floated into her head and clicked, as if it were meant. *This* was why today was special.

She went straight out, past Fred's baby carrier in the orchard, and right to the farthest corner of the garden. There, in a tangle of brier and elder, its felted roof curling and door hidden by nettles, was the old henhouse. It had stood there, henless, for as long as Posy could remember.

What Posy saw as she stood and gazed at it was a home—a home for a wandering bag lady. It was big enough. It even had windows; windows where Posy could see curtains, and perhaps a jug of flowers. It looked at least as big as the gingerbread house in her book about Hansel and Gretel.

"Perfect!" she breathed. "Brilling!"

For Posy Bates, to think was to act. She fetched the

shears from the garden shed and started to cut down the long grass and nettles. It was hard work.

Shall I get Sam to help? she wondered.

She decided not. The bag lady was hers, and private. Jealously, she remembered that the bag lady had given Sam the goldfish—the one Posy herself had given her only minutes before. She toiled on, hotter and hotter and stung all over her arms and legs. It was almost a relief when Fred began crying.

Posy dropped the shears and went to the carrier. She didn't want Daff to be interrupted in her search for things for the homeless.

The minute Fred saw her face bending over the carrier, he stopped yelling. Instead, he gurgled.

"Good boy," said Posy, gratified. And because she had a marvelous secret and was dying to share it, she told him about the bag lady and the henhouse.

"Listen, Fred," she said. "I've got this secret friend. I met her in the Victoria Center, and she's a bag lady!"

Fred gazed unwinkingly up at her. He could not possibly know how rare and exotic such a being was.

"Bag ladies are homeless," she told him. "They carry around everything they've got in bags. And they wander around the world carrying their bags and sleep under bridges, even when it snows."

Fred took this in very calmly.

"And *now* I've had this absolutely total idea!" Posy said. "I'm making a home for her in the old hen-

house. I'm going to sweep it out and put carpet down, and there'll be chairs and a jug of flowers and it'll be a dear little cottage!"

Fred shut his eyes, probably to try to imagine all this.

"I'm bound to see her again soon and then I'll tell her and she can move in straight away. Mom can't complain because she won't be under her feet, and, anyway, she'll be able to baby-sit. Yippee!"

Posy swooped under the hood and fished Fred out. She felt like throwing him into the air and catching him, like a ball, though fortunately she did not.

Daff *had* managed to find things for the homeless. Posy looked them over and was pleased.

That old wicker chair out of Pippa's room—that's ever so comfy to sit on. Oooh, and sheets and blankets—*and* a pillow. I'll have all of them. That rug and that table lamp. The henhouse was half finished already! She would get around later to thinking where the electricity would come from.

"That's ace, Mom," she told Daff. "Absolutely total. The homeless'll really like all this."

By "the homeless" she meant, of course, the bag lady.

"Good," said Daff. "I must say it must be terrible,

being homeless. Can hardly imagine it. Now I'm just off to the post office before it closes. If Fred starts crying, tell Pippa to get started on his feed."

She was off then, leaving the coast clear.

But I can't put them in the henhouse already, Posy thought. Haven't cleared the way to the door yet, and in any case it must be really dirty inside. Full of spiders, I should think.

A couple of weeks ago, this thought would have filled her with delight. Now, with the arrival of Buggins, spiders had rather paled.

She decided to move the donations into the potting shed. They would then not be under Daff's feet.

I'll tell her the Brownies are collecting later, she thought. True, anyway. Then, when I've got the henhouse clean, I can move things in when she's not looking.

Her plan was proceeding perfectly. She wished today could go on forever. She wished that by dark she could have the henhouse ready, all swept and clean with the rug down and the curtains up and a welcoming bunch of flowers. But she had to stop her preparations to go to Brownies.

Never mind, she thought. There'll be lots more stuff there.

There was. Miss Perlethorpe, who was even more

bossy when being Brown Owl than when being a teacher, made them all go around in pairs.

"You must ask politely," she told them. "Everything collected will be stored here in the hall, in the back room. You may bring any small items back with you, but do not attempt to move anything large or heavy. I myself have already brought along two items."

She indicated a hat stand and a cardboard box.

"What's in the box, miss?" asked Caroline Boot.

"Electric rollers," replied Miss Perlethorpe. "There is no reason why the homeless should not take pride in their appearance."

Posy, picturing the bag lady with a curly hairdo, snorted.

"You, Posy Bates, may well snigger," said Miss Perlethorpe quellingly. "One fine day we may see *you* with your hair properly brushed and combed. Now—into pairs. You, Posy, pair up with Mary Pye, who is at least sensible."

Mary Pye preened and Posy Bates glowered.

"Oh, gubbins!"

Grown-ups, she thought for the hundredth time, seemed to live in a different world. What she and her friends called goody-goody, grown-ups called sensible. They called tattletales responsible and know-it-alls intelligent. Mary Pye was all three of these rolled into one.

The two of them set off. Posy could not think of one single thing she wished to say to Mary Pye, so talked to herself instead.

Bet *she* never talks to bag ladies. Look at her little socks, white as snow! Bet she doesn't keep spiders in *her* bedroom. Bet her room's so tidy you could open it to the public and charge twenty-five cents. Bet *she'd* never live in a henhouse.

"My mother says if people are homeless, it's their own problem," said Mary.

Posy gritted her teeth and kept walking.

"She went to London last week and saw them. Said they were lying all over the place, all dirty and smelly."

Posy stopped dead in her tracks. Mary, surprised, stopped, too, and turned.

"*And* she's seen that dirty old woman Dick Martin saw, *and* she's called the police and reported her!"

Posy, who had stopped in order to take a few deep breaths and tell herself it was not a good idea to kick Mary, *did* kick her now. It was a hard one, full on the shin.

For an instant Mary goggled, disbelieving, and then, "*Eeeech!*" she let out a long scream. She turned and ran, sobbing, back toward the hall.

"Serve her right!" If Mrs. Pye had been there, Posy would probably have kicked her, too.

She turned and ran. She did not know where. All she knew was that she had to find her bag lady before the police did.

They'd take her bags! They'd put her in a cell!

The thought was unbearable. She could taste her own hot tears.

"I'll look everywhere! I'll look in every ditch and barn and behind every tree and hedge! I'll look all night!"

Posy Bates had forgotten that she was meant to be a Brownie doing a Good Deed. She was playing hide-and-seek instead. And this, she knew, was hide-and-seek in earnest. And she did not know whether she would still be playing it when the sun went down and darkness came with its bats and owls—and neither do you.

That is another story. . . .